Terry the Flying Turtle

by Anna Wilson

illustrated by Mike Gordon

Evans

CRJ

ZIG ZAG

First published by
Evans Brothers Limited
2A Portman Mansions
Chiltern St
London W1U 6NR

Reprinted 2007

British Library Cataloguing in Publication Data

Wilson, Anna
        Terry the Flying Turtle. - (Zig zags)
        1. Children's stories - Pictorial works
        I. Title
        823.9'14 [J]

ISBN 9780237527747

Printed in China by WKT Company Limited
Text copyright © Anna Wilson 2005
© in the illustrations Evans Brothers Ltd 2005

Series Editor: Nick Turpin
Design: Robert Walster
Production: Jenny Mulvanny
Series Consultant: Gill Matthews

"I'm clever," said Terry the Turtle. Polly the Chimp laughed.

Terry was cross.
"I **am** clever," said Terry.
"I can fly."

6

Polly laughed and laughed.
"You can't fly!" she said.

Terry was cross.
"I **can** fly," he said.
"You'll see."

"Will you help me?"
Terry asked the parrot.
"I want to fly."

The parrot
laughed.
Terry was cross.
"Please will
you help me?"
he asked.

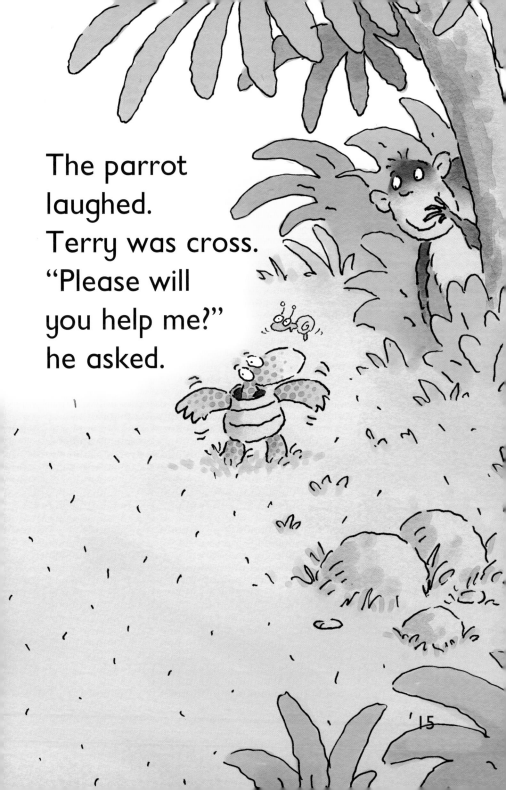

"Alright," said the parrot.
"Hold this twig and I'll
hold it too."

"Why?" asked Terry.

"Because it will help you fly," said the parrot.

The parrot held on.
Terry held on.

The parrot flew.
Terry flew!

The animals watched.
"Look at Terry!" they said.
"He looks silly!"

24

Terry was cross.
"I'm not silly," he shouted.
"You're silly. I'm flying!"

Terry fell
down and
down.

SPLASH!

"You look silly now!" Polly said.

Why not try reading another ZigZag book?

Dinosaur Planet ISBN 0 237 52793 6
by David Orme and Fabiano Fiorin

Tall Tilly ISBN 0 237 52794 4
by Jillian Powell and Tim Archbold

Batty Betty's Spells ISBN 0 237 52795 2
by Hilary Robinson and Belinda Worsley

The Thirsty Moose ISBN 0 237 52792 8
by David Orme and Mike Gordon

The Clumsy Cow ISBN 0 237 52790 1
by Julia Moffatt and Lisa Williams

Open Wide! ISBN 0 237 52791 X
by Julia Moffatt and Anni Axworthy

Too Small ISBN 0 237 52777 4
by Kay Woodward and Deborah van de Leijgraaf

I Wish I Was An Alien ISBN 0 237 52776 6
by Vivian French and Lisa Williams

The Disappearing Cheese ISBN 0 237 52775 8
by Paul Harrison and Ruth Rivers

Terry the Flying Turtle ISBN 0 237 52774 X
by Anna Wilson and Mike Gordon

Pet To School Day ISBN 0 237 52773 1
by Hilary Robinson and Tim Archbold

The Cat in the Coat ISBN 0 237 52772 3
by Vivian French and Alison Bartlett